Mia and the Magic Cupcakes

Written by Christina Dudley & Margo Engberg

Illustrated by Teri D. Sytsma

Mia and the Magic Cupcakes

Text copyright ©2010 by Christina Dudley and Margo Engberg

Illustrations copyright ©2010 by Teri D. Sytsma

Bella
VITA
www.bellavitapress.com

ISBN 978-0-983-07210-2

Cover and Book Design by

Kathy Campbell

Dedications

To Holly, Jackson and Lucy with all my love (C. D.)

To my "Littles": Gabe, Tycie, Jazzmyn, and Mia. You inspire me every day! (M. E.)

With hugs to my little Misses: Reya, Ellie and Audrey (T. S.)

Mia was small for her age.

"Eat your vegetables," her mother urged.
"So you can grow big and strong."

Mia wanted to grow big and strong.

But vegetables were
not very tempting.

She rejected rutabagas.

She balked at broccoli.

She loathed leeks.

She avoided asparagus.

She pooh-poohed peppers.

What Mia really loved was cupcakes.

"Cupcakes are treats, but they're not very nutritious," her mother said. "They won't make you big and strong."

Mia wanted to be big and strong.
But cupcakes were so very yummy.

She fancied frosting.

She cherished chocolate.

She pined for pineapple.

She swooned for swirls.

She melted for marshmallow.

Mia and her mother went to buy cupcakes for Mia's birthday picnic.

"I wish you had cupcakes that made you big and strong,"
Mia told the Bakery Lady. "My mother would let me eat
more cupcakes if they made you big and strong."

"We have every kind of cupcake there is," said the Bakery Lady.
"Eat this one for your birthday and see what happens."

At Mia's birthday picnic, her mother stuck a candle in the cupcake. "Make a wish, Mia."

"I wish this cupcake would make me big and strong!" thought Mia, and then she blew out the candle.

The first bite of the cupcake tasted like strawberries, and it made her think of summer days.

The second bite of the cupcake tasted like caramel, and it reminded her of hugs from grandma.

The third bite of the cupcake tasted like bananas and cream cheese, and Mia thought that, really, anything in the whole wide world could happen.

"Mia!" shrieked her mother.
"You're growing!" And she was.

Mia grew

and grew

and grew.

"Mama! Look how big and strong I am!" boomed Mia. "It's magic!"

At first, being enormous was fun. Everyone loved her.

She felt like a super hero.

But then it got a little tiresome.

She couldn't enjoy
her birthday presents.

It was hard to see the blackboard in class.

And Mrs. Chung never saw when she raised her hand.

Her friends didn't always want to play outside.

And she worried she might smoosh them.

Worst of all,
cupcakes were so tiny
she could barely
taste them.

Mia decided she better have a word with the Bakery Lady.

"I wish you had cupcakes that made you teeny-tiny," bellowed Mia. "This is a little too big and strong."

"We have every kind of cupcake there is," said the Bakery Lady. "Try a few dozen of these and see what happens."

The first dozen tasted like lemon cream, and they made her think of summer days.

The second dozen tasted like pineapple upside-down cake, and they reminded her of hugs from grandma.

The third dozen tasted like chocolate truffle, and Mia thought that, really, anything in the whole wide world could happen. "Mia!" she told herself, "You're shrinking!" And she was.

She shrank

and shrank

and shrank.

"I'm smaller than I was to begin with," marveled Mia. "It's magic!"

At first, being teeny-tiny was fun. Everyone loved her.

She felt adorable.

But then it got tiresome.

Her friends didn't always want to play dollhouse.

And she worried they might smoosh her.

The Bakery Lady used her to top cakes.

And plastic grooms don't talk much.

She even got bored of making frosting angels.

Worst of all, cupcakes were so giant to her she couldn't finish even one.

Mia decided she better have a word with the Bakery Lady.

"I wish you had cupcakes that made you just the right size," peeped Mia. "Even though I'm hungry for something else at this point."

"We have every kind of cupcake there is," said the Bakery Lady. "But no cupcake will make you exactly the right size. For that you need a variety of wholesome food."

Mia wanted to be just the right size. And other foods sounded interesting.

She sampled soups.

She popped pot stickers.

She checked out cheeses.

She nibbled nuts.

She experimented with eggplant.

Some of the foods she tried,

she *still* didn't care for.

But, over time, she grew back to her original size.

And even a little taller. And stronger. And faster.

"It's magic!" said Mia.

Best of all, cupcakes tasted wonderful again.

As special treats.

About the Authors

Christina Dudley is the author of novels *Mourning Becomes Cassandra* and *The Littlest Doubts* and one serious cupcake-aholic. She's even been known to buy a dozen and not let her three children know until they're half-gone. Her favorite? White cake with strawberry frosting. When she is behaving herself, she also blogs about local food and farms for the Bellevue Farmers Market as the UrbanFarmJunkie. For information on her books and speaking events—or just to see pictures of her standing next to cupcakes—check out **www.christinadudley.com**.

Margo Engberg is the mother of four adopted children and proud owner of Pinkabella™, a cute little cupcake shop with two locations. When not busy hauling kids here and there, or dreaming up and creating new cupcake flavors, Margo is driven by her passion for organizations dedicated to helping children in need!

CHRISTINA DUDLEY, MARGO ENGBERG & TERI SYTSMA

About the Illustrator

That blonde blur zipping past you wearing all those hats is Teri Sytsma, mother of three active girls. Between teaching art at her children's school, running Girl Scout troops, and shuttling back and forth to soccer games and practices, Teri indulges her passion for watercolors. Her gorgeous works have graced local public buildings, galleries, and private homes. For more information on her art, see **www.terisytsma.com**.